D0320863

Howling at the Moon

30130 149036856

For Bernadette
M. C.

To lovely Ben, up in the top of the tree
J. N.

First published in Great Britain in 2006 by Gullane Children's Books
This paperback edition published in 2007 by

Gullane Children's Books,
an imprint of Alligator Books

Winchester House, 259-269 Old Marylebone Road,

London NW1 5XJ

1 3 5 7 9 10 8 6 4 2

Text © Michael Catchpool 2006
Illustrations © Jill Newton 2006

The right of Michael Catchpool and Jill Newton to be identified as the author and illustrator of this work
has been asserted by them in accordance with the Copyright, Designs and Patents Act, 1988.
A CIP record for this title is available from the British Library.

ISBN-13: 978-1-86233-678-0
All rights reserved. No part of this publication may be reproduced,
stored in a retrieval system, or transmitted in any form or by any means,
electronic, mechanical, photocopying, recording or otherwise, without prior permission.

Printed and bound in China

The night was dark. The moon was high. From up on the hill came a sound.

H…o…o…o…w…w…l!

'W-what's that noise?' chirped two owl chicks from
their nest at the top of the tall tree.
'That,' said their mother, 'sounds
like a wolf, howling at the moon!'
'A wolf – what's a wolf?' asked the chicks, their eyes
big and wide, 'And why does it howl?'

'Ah, an awful thing is a wolf,' said their mother peering this way
and that. 'Keep away from a wolf – it has terrible teeth and
scratchy claws. And it howls because it is so hungry!'
'We'll definitely keep away from a wolf,' agreed the chicks.
'Very wise,' said their mother.

Just below, three young squirrels,
(who should have been in bed),
chased each other round and
round the trunk, when
suddenly, through the
trees they heard . . .

H…o…o…o…w…w…l!

'What was that?' they chattered, their noses twitching and their tails all bushy. 'Now that,' said an old, grey squirrel, peering out from the drey, 'that sounds like a wolf, howling at the moon.'

'A wolf – what's a wolf and why does it howl?' asked the three young squirrels, huddling close together on a branch.

'Well I've heard,' said the old grey squirrel, 'that wolves have got terrible teeth and scratchy claws . . . and there's more – they've got cold yellow eyes and a spiky old tail. They're mean and they're cruel. And they howl because they're so angry – so I've heard. Don't go near a wolf!'

'Oh, we won't,' agreed the three young squirrels and they nipped inside to bed.

Further down, four little mice played
hide-and-seek amongst the roots.
They scuttled up and down
until suddenly
they heard . . .
H...o...o...o...o...w...w...l!

'Did you hear
that?' they squeaked
to each other. 'What ever can it be?'
'Now that,' said their father with his whiskers
twitching, 'sounds like a wolf, howling at the moon!'

'But what's a wolf like?' asked the little mice, 'And why does it howl?'
'I'll tell you a thing or two about a wolf,' said their father. 'I've heard they've got
terrible teeth and scratchy claws, cold yellow eyes and a spiky old tail . . .

and there's more.
They've got nasty hair
as sharp as thorns. And
they howl because they are
so terribly, terribly grumpy!
Never get close to a wolf.'

'We definitely won't get close to a wolf,'
said the little mice as they scurried
inside a hollow log . . .

first one,

then another . . .

and another . . .
and another . . .

'Very sensible too,' said their
father who popped inside to join them.

Until all that was left was . . .

one little mouse who was fast asleep, curled up tight in a cosy little ball.

Suddenly, through the

night there came a sound . . .

H...o...o...o...o...w...w...l!

'What ever's that?' said the sleepy mouse
waking up with a stretch and a yawn.
But there was no-one to tell him . . .

so he went to find out!

Past the trees with their twisty branches, he went.

H...o...o...o...W...W...l!

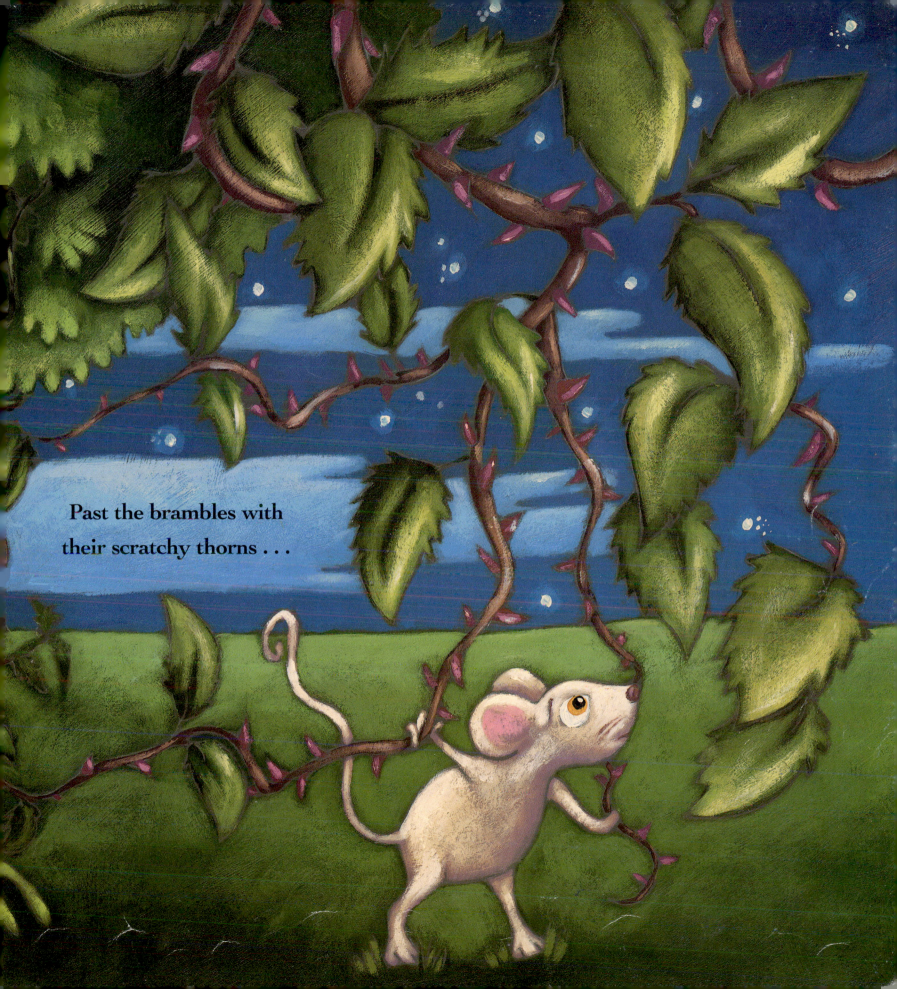

Past the brambles with
their scratchy thorns . . .

H…o…o…o…o…w…w…l!

Past the bushes with
their juicy berries . . .

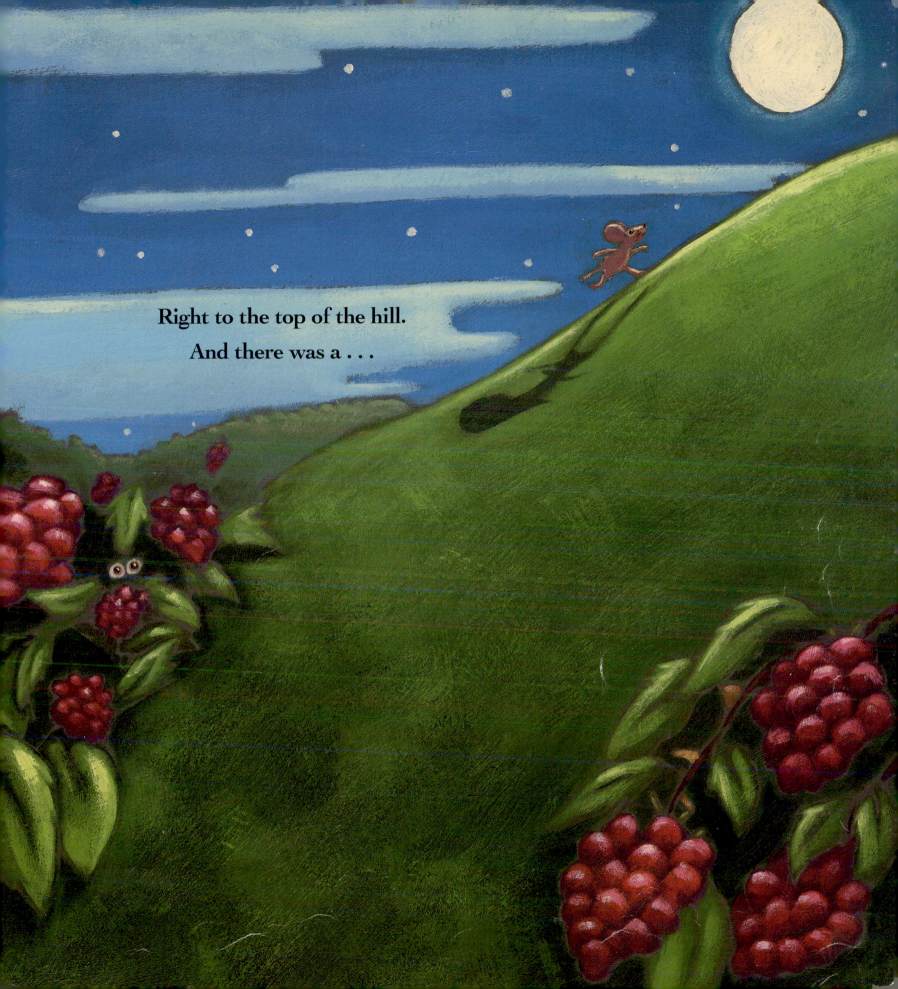

Right to the top of the hill.

And there was a . . .

A small, grey wolf howling . . .
and howling . . . as the moon shone high.

?...w...w...l!

'Who are you?' asked the sleepy mouse getting very
close to the wolf, very close indeed.
'I'm a wolf!' said the wolf.'
'And why do you howl?' asked the sleepy mouse,
so close he could almost touch the wolf and the
wolf could almost touch him. 'Are you hungry?
Are you angry? Are you grumpy?'
The wolf shook his head.
'No, I howl,' said the wolf,
        'because . . .

because . . . I'm lonely
and I've no-one to play with.'

The sleepy mouse stretched out a paw – a tiny paw, and touched the wolf.
And gently, very gently, stroked his soft fur.

'I might be small, and you might be big, but I
could be your friend.'
'Could you really?' said the wolf.
'I think I could. I really think I could,' said the
mouse looking into the wolf's warm, kind eyes.

And the two of them rolled and tumbled . . .

And hid and found . . .

And laughed as they chased each other through the bushes . . .
By the brambles . . . Under the branches . . .

Round the tall tree – past the wide, surprised eyes . . .

H....o....o....o....W....W....

Squ...eak...Squ....eak

and back to the hill-top
where they howled and
squeaked and squeaked and
howled at the moon because
they were both so . . .

The end.